9:30

9:42

JACK and the WHOOPEE WIND

written by **MARY CALHOUN** *illustrated by* **DICK GACKENBACH**

William Morrow & Co., Inc./New York

William Morrow and Company, Inc.,
105 Madison Avenue,
New York, NY 10016.
Printed in Hong Kong.
1 2 3 4 5 6 7 8 9 10
Library of Congress Cataloging-in-Publication Data
Calhoun, Mary.
Jack and the whoopee wind.
Summary: Mad at the wind for blowing everything
away, Jack tries a succession of ways to stop it.
[1. Wind—Fiction.   2. Tall tales]   I. Gackenbach,
Dick, ill.   II. Title.
PZ7.C1278Jac 1987   [E]   86-16360
ISBN 0-688-06137-0
ISBN 0-688-06138-9 (lib. bdg.)

To Koben and Copper,
who helped make this story

Jack liked a breeze now and then, but where he lived in Whoopee, Wyoming, people had to tie down their cats so they didn't blow away. He lived on a farm, except that most of it had blown away. The chickens were bald, and the wind had scooped up the fence posts and sprinkled them on the prairie.

Jack had a long-legged dog named Mose, and when the wind tormented his dog, Jack began to get mad. One day as Mose was chasing a rabbit, the wind whisked them up and sailed them away.

"That pesky wind!" Jack yelled. "It took my dog!"

He shook his fist, but the Whoopee wind just swirled around his head.

After Jack got his dog and the rabbit untangled, Mose walked bent kneed, close to the ground. He was a most embarrassed dog. At the house he crawled under the porch and stayed there.

Jack hated to see his good old dog beaten down like that.
Next morning he called under the porch, "Come on, Mose.
I'm gonna stop that wind!"

He brought out a big fan, hooked it up with long cords and pointed it into the wind.

"There!" said Jack. "That'll shove back the wind." He turned on the fan. Whirr went the fan, but whoosh went the wind, and the fan tipped over.

Mose barked, but the wind blew away the sound. Way beyond the barn it came out, "Yarp! Yarp!"

Then Jack declared war on the wind. "You may be bigger than I am," he yelled, "but I mean business!"

Jack and his dog took off down the road toward town with the wind snickering around them. He got all the kids in Whoopee, and they got all their bedsheets. "We'll catch the wind in a bundle," Jack said, "and drop it in the gully."

They made a great wind sock with the sheets, and it filled with wind and tumbled over the edge.

But the Whoopee wind kept right on blowing.

Jack saw he'd have to be smarter than the wind. So he
studied it — how the wind hustled to catch its tail, how it
gusted dust in the the sky, how it whistled straight across
Whoopee until people's nerves stood on end.

Jack figured it out. The problem was the Windy Hills west of
town. Between the hills was Windy Gap, and that's where the
wind got all pushed together and pointed at Whoopee. The
thing to do was to plug up Windy Gap.

"Come on, Mose," Jack called. "I've got a plan."

Jack rounded up all the cowboys, who brought all the
blankets in Whoopee County. And they all rode up to Windy
Gap, where they sewed the blankets into a huge curtain. With
their lariats they made a long rope and hung the curtain
between the hills.

The wind pushed against the curtain and fell back.

"We've stopped that pesky wind!" Jack cried.

But the wind took a bigger huff and ducked under the curtain, rolling Jack and the cowboys like tumbleweeds. The cowboys started for home.

"Now, wait," Jack said. "I've got another idea. We're gonna stop that everlasting wind!"

On the edge of town stood an old outdoor movie screen.
Jack and the cowboys loaded it on a big flatbed truck, and
they drove to the Windy Hills, where they set up the screen.
"Now the wind can't get through Windy Gap," said Jack.

Sure enough, the wind couldn't blow through the screen. Instead, it scooted up over the screen, high in the sky, landed —*whap*—on the Whoopee town jail, and caved in the roof. Luckily nobody was in there.

"That wind just blows where it wants to!" a cowboy said in disgust.

"I've got it!" Jack said. "We'll build a U-shaped tunnel. The wind will blow in one end and out the other. We'll shoot that wind back where it came from!"

Jack and the cowboys got everybody in town to bring their shovels, and they started digging two holes into one of the Windy Hills. Mose helped, pawing up dirt and kicking it out.

The wind helped, too. It whooshed into both holes and bored them bigger. But about the time the diggers met at the back of the tunnel, the wind met itself coming. There was such a ruckus of wind back there that the top of the hill blew off, tossing everyone in the air.

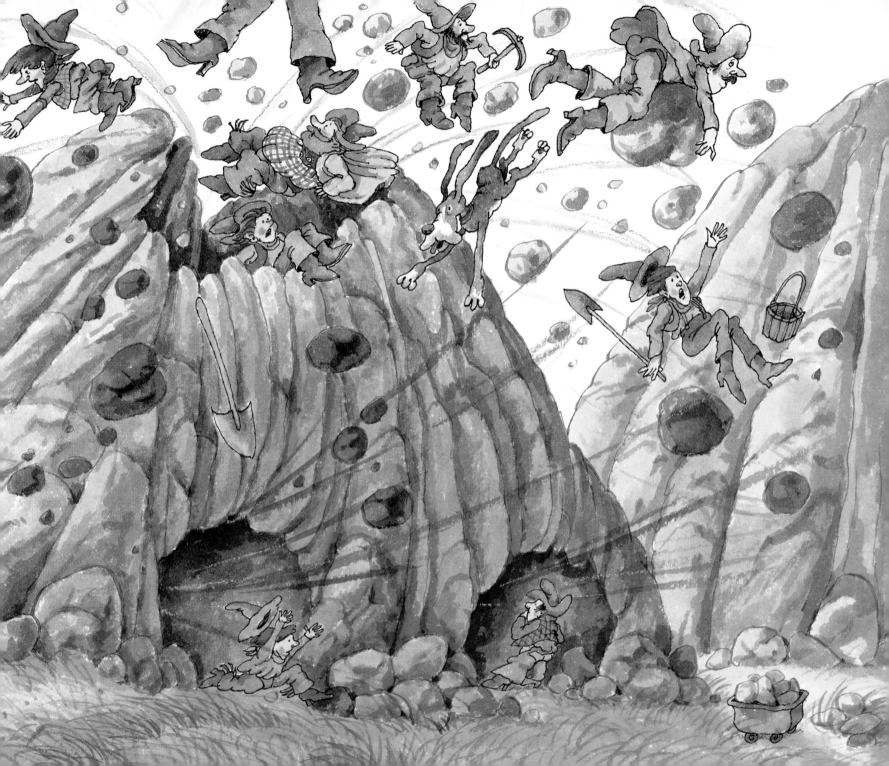

"I declare!" cried a cowboy. "The trouble with that wind is it hasn't got enough to do!"

"That's it!" Jack shouted. "If we can't stop the wind, we'll use it!"

He got the cowboys to bring all the scrap metal in the state of Wyoming.

"What are we building?" asked the cowboys.

"Wait and see," said Jack.

When they were done, they had planted a forest of windmills at the bottom of Windy Gap. Each one was hooked up to a machine that turned out electricity.

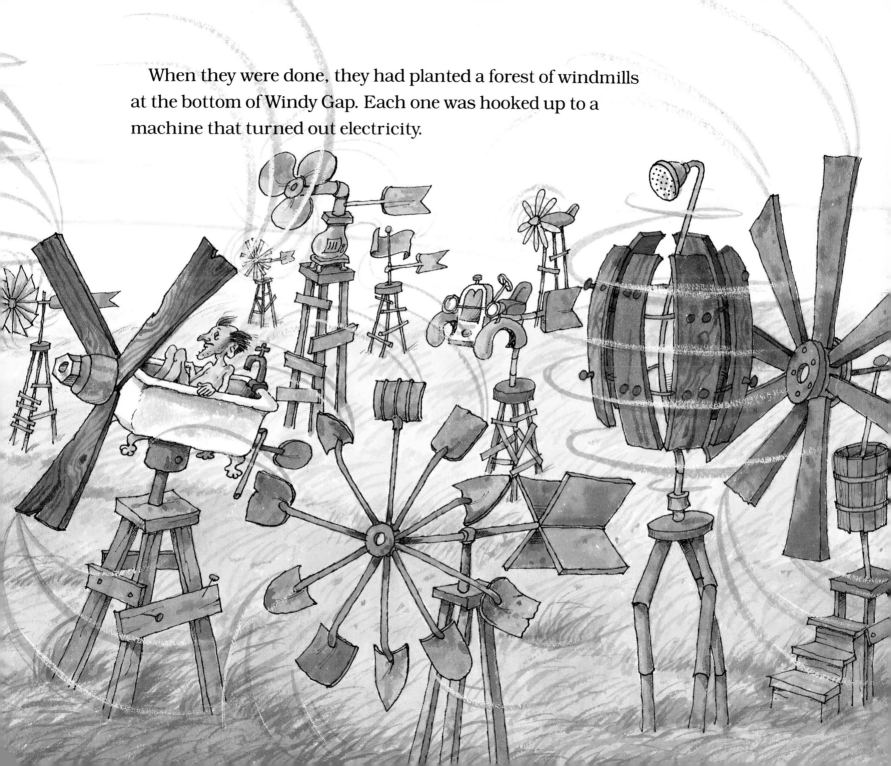

Well, it worked. The wind hurried down the Gap and got all caught up in whirling blades and barrels. The wind huffed the mills, and the mills made electricity, and everybody in Whoopee got rich. The Whoopee wind was so busy spinning windmills that only a little trickled down over town.

So Mose snoozed in the sunshine, and seldom did a whisk of wind lift his ears. And when the air hummed with a soft breeze, Jack just grinned.

After all, it wouldn't be Whoopee, Wyoming, without wind.